Welcome
aboard!
ign below, and
u'll be an official
member of the
Salty Dogs.

For my brothers James, Richard, and Buster.

OXFORD
UNIVERSITY PRESS

Great Clarendon Street, Oxford OX2 6DP
Oxford University Press is a department of the University of Oxford.
It furthers the University's objective of excellence in research, scholarship,
and education by publishing worldwide. Oxford is a registered trade mark of
Oxford University Press in the UK and in certain other countries

Text and illustrations copyright © Matty Long 2017
The moral rights of the author and illustrator have been asserted
Database right Oxford University Press (maker)
First published 2017

British Library Cataloguing in Publication Data

Data available
ISBN: 978-0-19-274865-2 (paperback)
ISBN: 978-0-19-274866-9 (eBook)

1 3 5 7 9 10 8 6 4 2

Printed in China

Far off in a distant ocean lie the Pirate Islands, where swords are drawn and ships are sunk all in the name of TREASURE.

Among the fearsome pirates battling for treasure are . . .

And the Salty Dogs.

With the wind in their sails, the Salty Dogs set off. But the Green Shell Gang was paying the Crazy Horn Crew a visit. Getting past them might be tricky.

Captain Fifi was running a tight ship.

Spirits were high as the Salty Dogs neared Crossbone Island.

Captain Fifi's crew doggy paddled like they had never doggy paddled before.

And with their journey to Crossbone Island finally complete...

The Sea Monkey captain had a mutiny on his hand.

The Salty Dogs saw their chance.
The treasure was there for the taking.

With the *Scoundrel* under new ownership, the Sea Monkeys
were left shipless and stranded on Crossbone Island.

And for the Salty Dogs . . .

... treasure never tasted so good.